USBORNE FIRST READING
Level Three

USBORNE FIRST READING

The **Dinosaur** Who Lost His **ROAR**

Russell Punter
Illustrated by Andy Elkerton

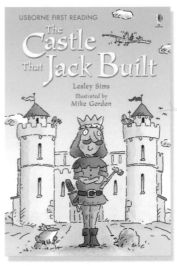

USBORNE FIRST READING

The **Castle** That **Jack Built**

Lesley Sims
Illustrated by Mike Gordon

USBORNE FIRST READING

Chicken Licken

retold by
Russell Punter
Illustrated by Ann Kronheimer

USBORNE FIRST READING

The **Three Little Pigs**

retold by
Susanna Davidson
Illustrated by Georgien Overwater

The Castle That Jack Built

Lesley Sims

Illustrated by
Mike Gordon

Reading Consultant: Alison Kelly
Roehampton University

This story is about

Jack

a castle

some gold

a dragon

a wagon

a witch

a troll

a frog

a girl

and a prince.

This is the castle that
Jack built.

This is the gold

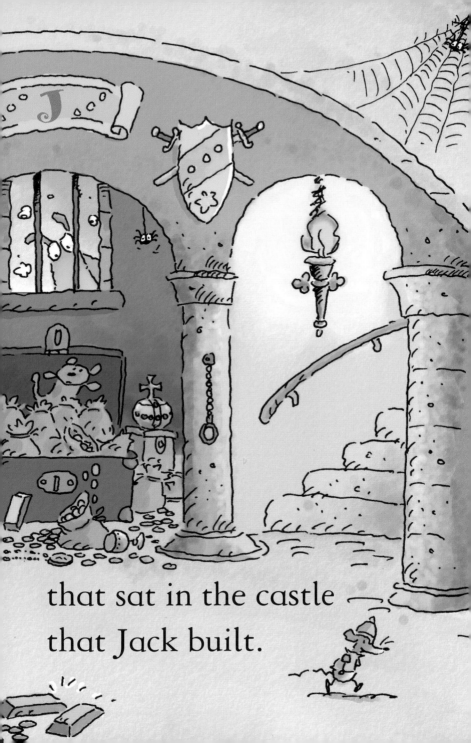

that sat in the castle
that Jack built.

This is the dragon who stole the gold

that sat in the castle
that Jack built.

This is the
wagon that
followed the dragon

who stole the gold

that sat in the castle
that Jack built.

This is the witch

who sat in the wagon

that followed the dragon
who stole the gold

that sat in the castle
that Jack built.

who upset the witch
who sat in the wagon

that followed the dragon
who stole the gold

that sat in the castle
that Jack built.

This is the wagon turned upside down

tipped by the troll
with the scritchy itch

21

who upset the witch
who sat in the wagon

that followed the dragon
who stole the gold

that sat in the castle
that Jack built.

This is the frog
with a grumpy frown

who hopped from
the wagon turned
upside down

tipped by the troll
with the scritchy itch

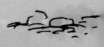

who upset the witch
who sat in the wagon

that followed the dragon

who stole the gold

that sat in the castle
that Jack built.

This is the girl
in a silver gown

who kissed the frog
with a grumpy frown

who hopped from
the wagon turned
upside down

tipped by the troll
with the scritchy itch

who upset
the witch

who sat in
the wagon

33

that followed the dragon

who stole the gold

that sat in the castle
that Jack built.

This is the prince
who came to town

and kissed the girl in a
silver gown.

He was the frog with a
grumpy frown

who hopped from
the wagon turned
upside down

tipped by the troll
with the scritchy itch

who upset the witch
who sat in the wagon

39

that followed the dragon

who stole the gold

that sat in the castle
that Jack built.

This is King Jack
with his golden crown.

His son is the prince
who came to town

and kissed the girl
in a silver gown.

And they all lived
happily ever after,

safe in the castle that
Jack built.

Digital illustration by Carl Gordon
Designed by Louise Flutter
With thanks to Lottie Sims, aged 6, for her comments

First published in 2007 by Usborne Publishing Ltd., Usborne House,
83-85 Saffron Hill, London EC1N 8RT, England. www.usborne.com
Copyright © 2007 Usborne Publishing Ltd.

48

USBORNE FIRST READING
Level Four

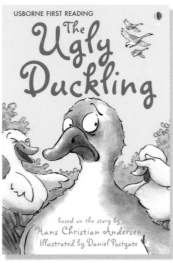

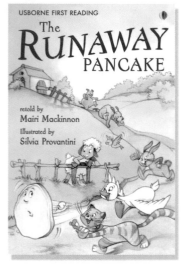